Agnes
and the Hen

For my four little Rosies ~ E.R.

For Bonnie, Joe, and Eliza x ~ C.T.G.

DK | Penguin Random House

Author Elle Rowley
Illustrator Clare Therese Gray

Editor Laura Gilbert
Senior Designer Elle Ward
Editorial Assistant Kieran Jones
Senior Production Editor Nikoleta Parasaki
Production Controller Leanne Burke
Jacket Coordinator Magda Pszuk
Publisher Francesca Young
Deputy Art Director Mabel Chan
Publishing Director Sarah Larter

First published in Great Britain in 2024 by
Dorling Kindersley Limited
DK, One Embassy Gardens, 8 Viaduct Gardens, London, SW11 7BW

The authorised representative in the EEA is
Dorling Kindersley Verlag GmbH. Arnulfstr. 124, 80636 Munich, Germany

Text copyright © 2024 Elle Rowley
Design and illustration copyright © 2024 Dorling Kindersley Limited
A Penguin Random House Company
10 9 8 7 6 5 4 3 2 1
001–326764–Jan/2024

A CIP catalogue record for this book is available from the British Library.
ISBN: 978-0-2415-3611-7

Printed and bound in China

MIX
Paper | Supporting
responsible forestry
FSC™ C018179

This book was made with Forest
Stewardship Council™ certified
paper – one small step in DK's
commitment to a sustainable future.
For more information go to
www.dk.com/our-green-pledge

www.dk.com

Agnes
and the Hen

Written by
Elle Rowley

Illustrated by
Clare Therese Gray

On a little farm, behind a medium-sized cottage, lived a big dog named Agnes. She was strong and wise (most of the time) and she was a friend to all. More than anything, Agnes loved to be cosy.

Agnes had many jobs on the farm. Every night, she locked the chickens up in their coop before making her way to the cottage to sleep.

This kept the hens safe from sneaky foxes.

The hens were rather tidy and orderly hens
(most of the time).

They went about their lives
in the same way every day,
laying their eggs in their
nesting boxes at
the same time
each morning,

cluck cluck cluck cluck

marching and clucking perfectly as one,

pecking and scratching at
the dirt in straight lines,

and sleeping in a
perfect row inside
the coop at night.

Everyone but Rosie, that is.

Rosie was the smallest hen and she was different from the other hens.

Rosie was not exactly disorderly, but she was definitely not orderly like the others. She laid her eggs whenever and wherever it suited her.

She wandered all over, usually following Agnes, dancing, howling like a dog, and catching bugs in the air wherever she went.

And, most shockingly, instead of sleeping with the other hens each night, Rosie slept above them on the branch of a tree.

Rosie may have been different from her friends, but she didn't notice. She was a happy hen.

Until, one day, she wasn't.

After days of rain, the sun shone brightly on the farm.
Rosie was so excited that her legs and wings began to move
and, soon, she was dancing right through the chicken yard.

She was dancing with such energy that she rolled down the hill,

landing in a muddy puddle, waking Agnes from a cosy nap.

Agnes gently nudged Rosie out of the muddy puddle and walked Rosie back to the coop.

Agnes and Rosie found the other hens looking down at the ground, pecking in their perfect rows by the coop as they always did.

As Rosie got closer,
the hens stopped pecking
and stared at her. They
looked disapprovingly
at Rosie's feathers.

Then, without a word, the hens turned their tail feathers away from Rosie and started pecking all together once more.

For the first time, Rosie felt alone. Rosie wondered
if being different from the other hens was a bad
thing. She slumped down on a nesting box
where no one could see her.

The other hens continued on without noticing, but Agnes, who noticed just about everything, walked over to Rosie. Agnes didn't say anything at first. She just stood by her. Then, Agnes whispered,

"Not all who are different are lost,
Losing yourself has the greater cost."

For a moment,
Rosie's heart lifted
at the words.

At sundown, the hens all gathered to the coop
door, right on schedule. Agnes wished everyone
a cosy good night as Rosie hopped through
the coop roof to her tree.

Right before Agnes shut the
latch, it caught on a little,
splintered piece of wood,
stopping it from closing fully.

Excited to get to
her cosy featherbed
in the cosy cottage,
Agnes didn't notice,
and quickly walked
down to the house.

Late that night, when the moon hung low and the hens were sound asleep, two foxes circled the farm like they always did at night. Right away they saw the open latch. They ran to the door, jumping up to lift it.

Rosie heard their rattling
from her tree branch and
knew something
was wrong.

Rosie was afraid, but she knew what she must do. She hopped through the hole in the roof, waking the hens up with a start.

Rosie motioned to them to follow. Silently but swiftly, the hens pushed through the hole and hopped right up to Rosie's branch, just as the foxes opened the door.

The foxes were quite confused, but
they were not giving up that easily.

The hens froze.

As the foxes approached, Rosie had another
idea. She began howling like a dog.

Alarmed, the foxes stood still. The hens, seeing their shock, quickly joined in, creating a loud howling chorus.

Mistaking their howling for dogs, the foxes
shot up in a flurry, racing to the gate to escape.

Their howling was so
loud that it roused Agnes in
the cottage. She bolted up to the
coop, adding her deep howl to
theirs, but the foxes were
already gone.

The hens rejoiced in their victory
and Rosie beamed.

Giving up her own cosy bed, Agnes slept on
the dirt by the coop the rest of the night,
just in case the foxes returned.

The next morning, Rosie slept in later than usual, tired from the long night.

She looked down below to see the other hens, who had already started on their day, pecking in straight lines, but as she looked closer...

...she could see their legs shifting and moving, dancing as they pecked.